This book belongs to.

who is loved by
SISTERS,
FRIENDS &
FAMILY
every day!

To the sisters we are born with and
the sisters we make along the way.
May we always have each other's back!

Copyright © 2022 by Mechal Renee Roe

All rights reserved. Published in the United States by Doubleday,
an imprint of Random House Children's Books, a division of Penguin Random House LLC, New York.

Doubleday is a registered trademark and the Doubleday colophon is a trademark of Penguin Random House LLC.
HAPPY HAIR is a registered trademark of Happy Hair.

Visit us on the Web! rhcbooks.com

Educators and librarians, for a variety of teaching tools, visit us at
RHTeachersLibrarians.com

Library of Congress Cataloging-in-Publication Data
Name: Roe, Mechal Renee, author, illustrator.
Title: Smart sisters / written & illustrated by Mechal Renee Roe.
Description: First edition. | New York : Doubleday Books for Young Readers, [2022] |
Series: Happy hair. | Audience: Ages 3–7.
Summary: "A celebration of sisterhood and friendship, told in positive
affirmations spoken by Black and Brown girls sporting natural hairstyles"
—Provided by publisher.
Identifiers: LCCN 2022005795 (print) | LCCN 2022005796 (ebook) |
ISBN 978-0-593-43318-8 (hardcover) | ISBN 978-0-593-43319-5 (library binding) |
ISBN 978-0-593-43320-1 (ebook)
Subjects: CYAC: Stories in rhyme. | Hair—Fiction. | Hairstyles—Fiction. |
LCGFT: Stories in rhyme. | Picture books.
Classification: LCC PZ8.3.R6185 Sm 2023 (print) |
LCC PZ8.3.R6185 (ebook) | DDC [E]—dc23

MANUFACTURED IN CHINA
10 9 8 7 6 5 4 3 2 1
First Edition

A
HAPPY HAIR®
BOOK

SMART SISTERS

Written & illustrated by MECHAL RENEE ROE

Doubleday Books
for Young Readers

STAR LIGHT, STAR BRIGHT!

my sister and me!

TWO OF A KIND SHARPENS THE MIND!

my sister and me!

NOT AFRAID TO ASK WHY!
ALWAYS WILLING TO TRY!

my sister and me!

ACTIONS ARE BOLD!
LOVE IS GOLD!

my sister and me!

INSPIRE AND DREAM!

WE MAKE A GREAT TEAM!

my sister and me!

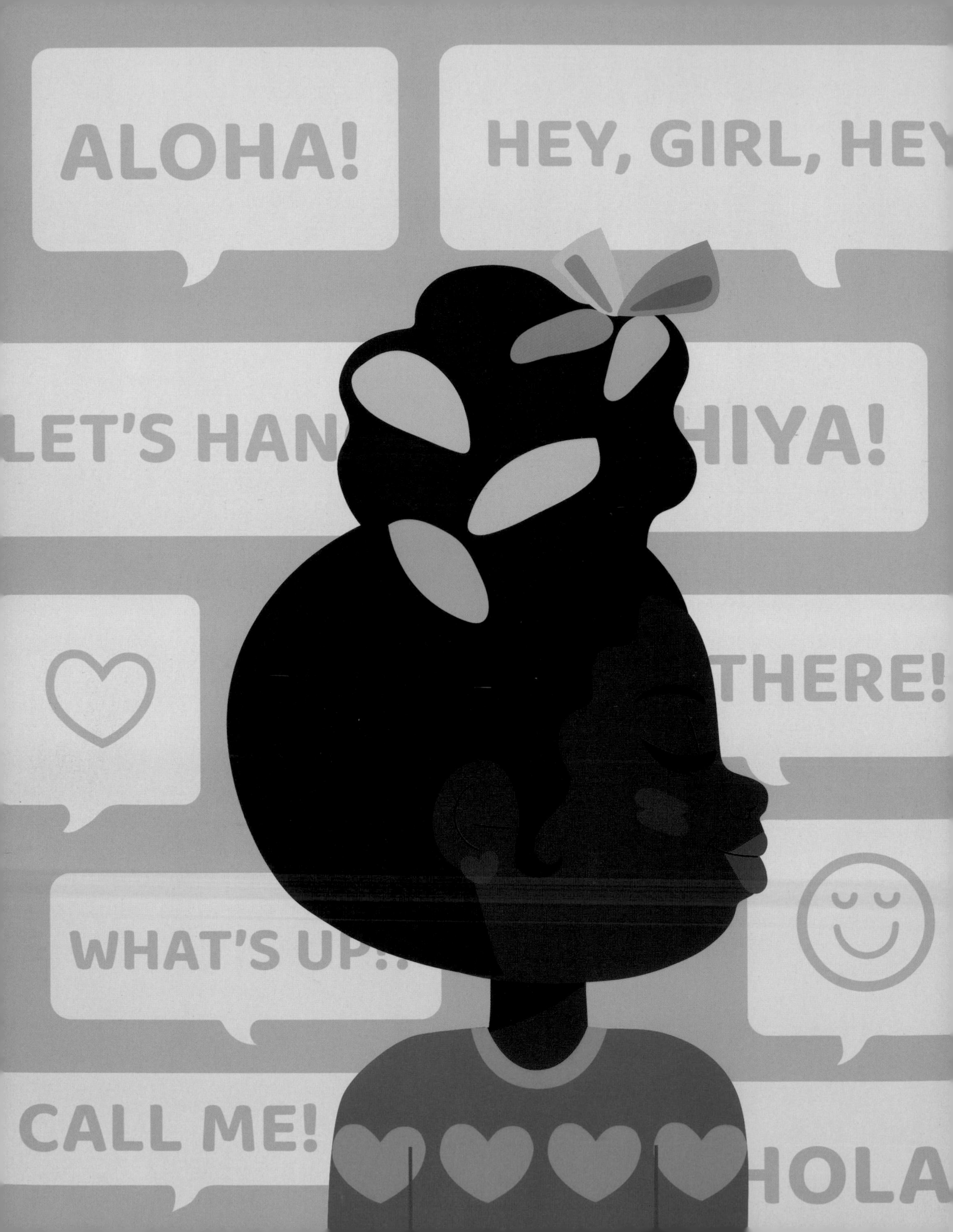
ALOHA!
HEY, GIRL,
HIYA!
THERE!
WHAT'S UP
CALL ME!

WHEN IN DOUBT, GIVE HER A SHOUT!

my sister and me!

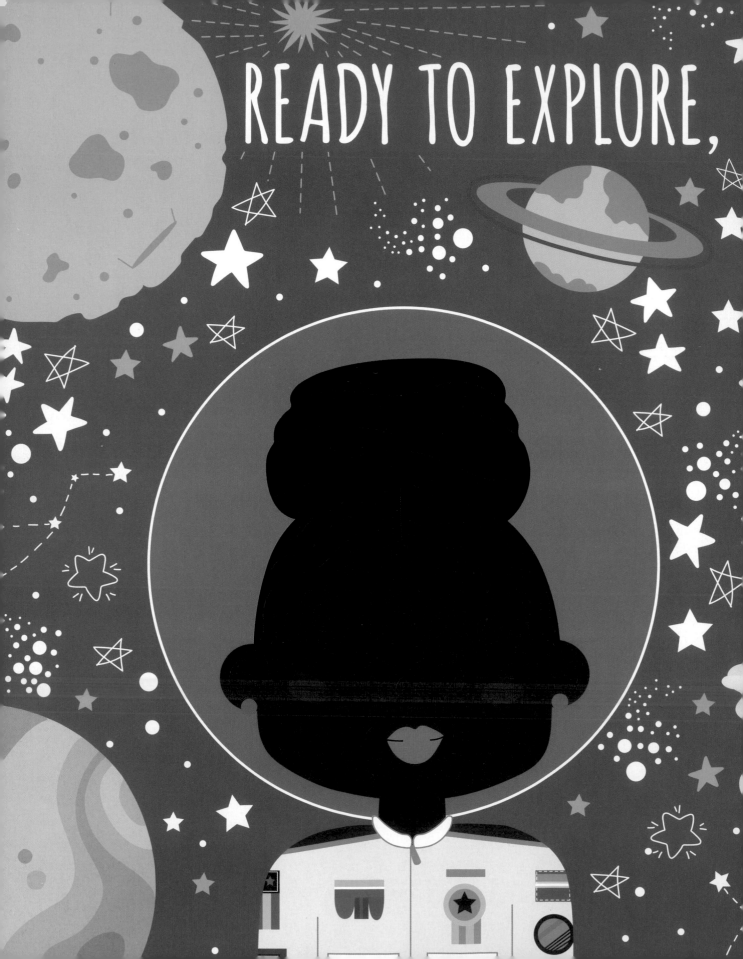

SWEET AND KIND,
A VERY RARE FIND!

my sister and me!

REGAL AND ROYAL, LOVELY AND LOYAL!

my sister and me!

SHE HAS MY BACK!
KEEPS ME ON TRACK!

my sister and me!

PERFECT TOGETHER! ALWAYS AND FOREVER!

my sister and me!

SISTERS ARE FRIENDS FOR LIFE!

A
HAPPY HAIR®
BOOK